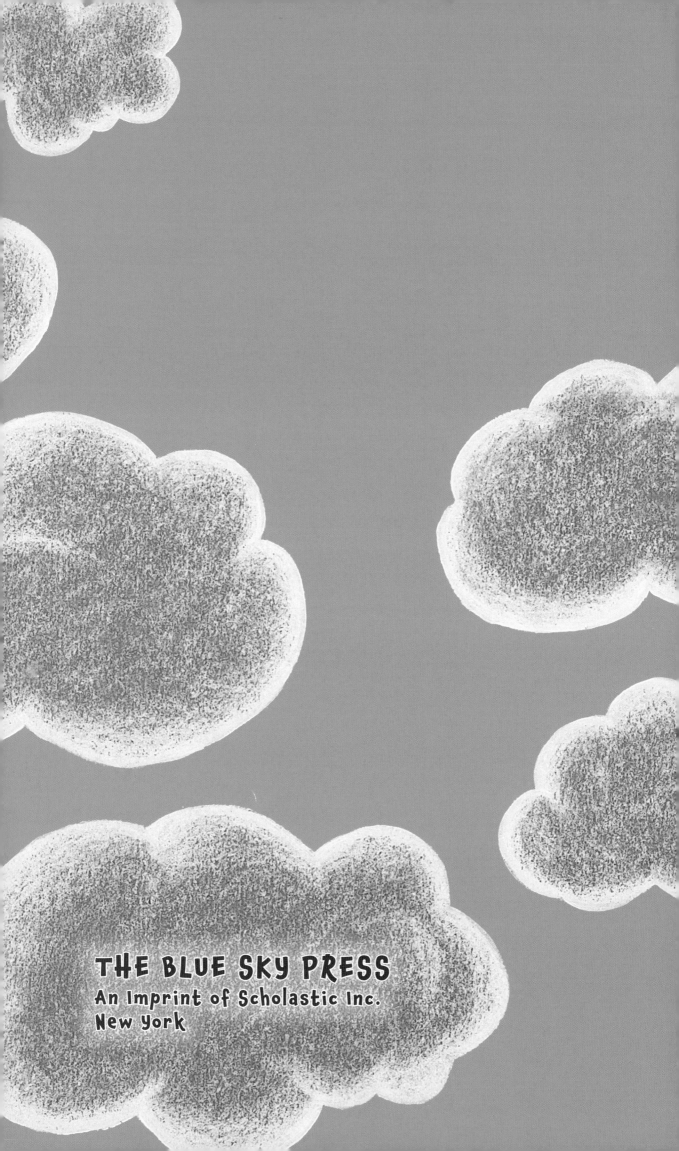

THE BLUE SKY PRESS

An Imprint of Scholastic Inc.
New York

BLUE SKY

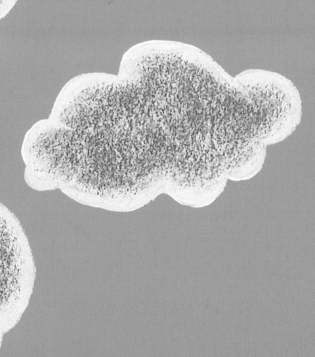

Audrey Wood

Library of Congress catalog card number: 2011010374
ISBN 978-0-545-31610-1
10 9 8 7 6 5 4 3 2 1   12 13 14 15 16
Printed in Singapore   46
First printing, March 2012

For
Bruce Wood

BLUE

Sky

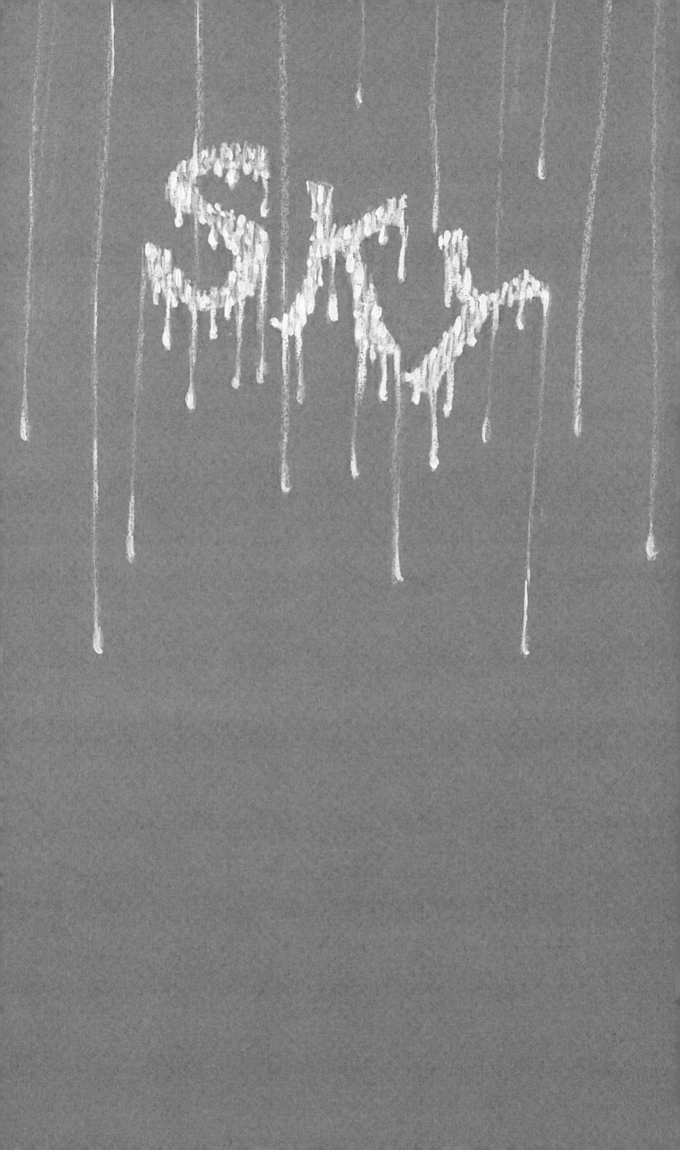

SUNSET

MOON

SKY

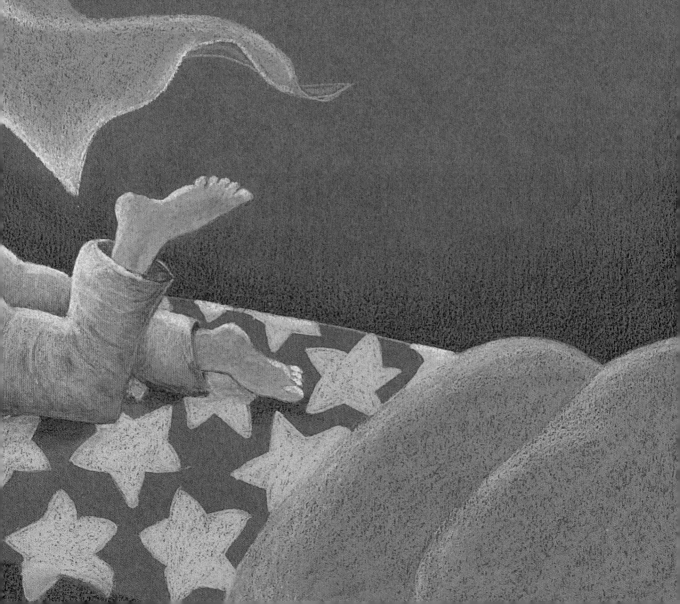

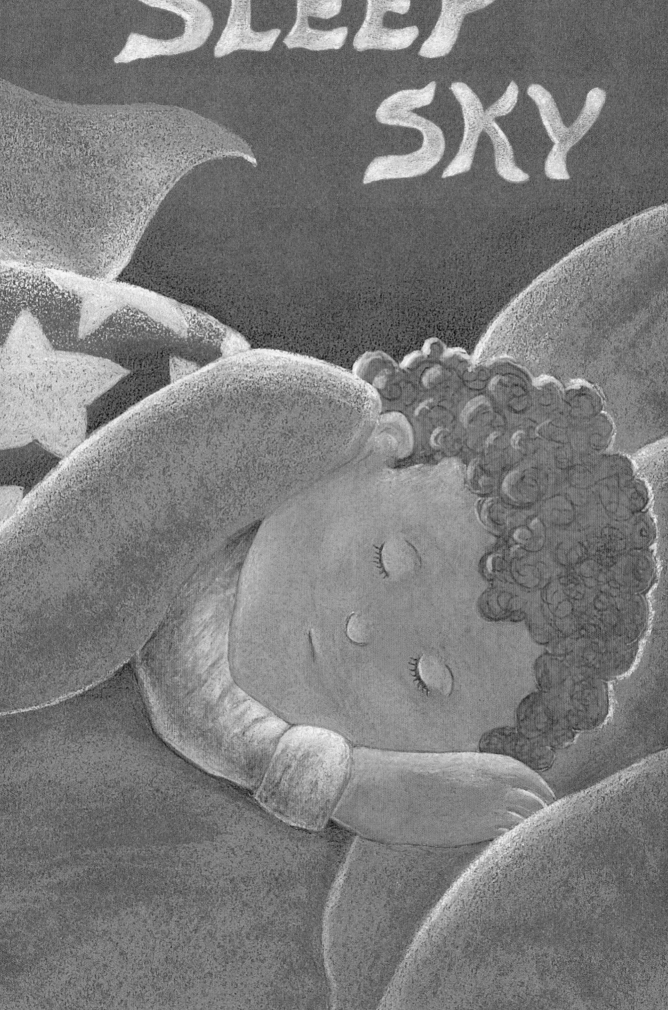